Jinx and tale of Lanky the Lemur

Written by Steven Narleski
Illustrated by Steven Narleski and Leanne Tursi
Copyright © 2014

Gather round for a tale of tails!
A story of friends from different trails!

Listen close so you can hear,
how two unlikely friends held each other dear.

But wait! A dog and a lemur? What's that you say?
I don't believe it! It can't be! No way!

Yet it happened just like this.
It happened I say!

A dog and a lemur, still friends to this day!

They played basketball,

hockey,

soccer and catch.

They rode skateboards,

bicycles, flew kites and played fetch.

Always good times. They hung out a bunch!
Then when school started, they sat together at lunch.

If you saw them together,
you'd think he was her brother.
Except Lanky the Lemur didn't look like the others.

But Jinx didn't mind. Never gave it a thought.
Until one day on the playground, she was distraught.

Billy the bulldog said,
"Look at that lemur...so skinny and tall!
He looks so silly and can't bark at all!"

"Why do you play with him, Jinx?
Lanky looks like a fool."

"Yeah, hang out with us Jinx,
or we'll think you're not cool!"

Just then the bell rang,
it was the end of recess.

But Jinx couldn't focus on school...
she had a feeling of stress.

Jinx thought, "Why would they make fun of Lanky? Lemurs are fun!"

She couldn't think of a reason... not any...not ONE!

Now Jinx wanted to fit in... what dog doesn't?

But Lanky was her friend... she couldn't imagine if he wasn't!

Jinx thought for a minute and ran her paws through her fur.

She had to stick up for Lanky...
he would do it for her!

The next day at the bus stop it started again.
Billy poked and prodded, making fun of her friend.

Jinx spoke calm and clear. Her voice showed no doubt.
She looked right at Billy and let her true feelings out.
"Lanky is my friend...I don't care what anyone thinks.
If I worried about that I'd be YOU and not JINX!"

"You have your opinion...
that's fine I suppose.

But you wouldn't know fun
if it landed on your nose."

The other dogs laughed, and Jinx smiled inside.

The bus pulled up,
and they got on for their ride.

That day at recess when Jinx and Lanky started to play,

A few more dogs came jumping their way.

"We think you're right Jinx!
Those dogs aren't any fun!"

They only care about fancy clothes,

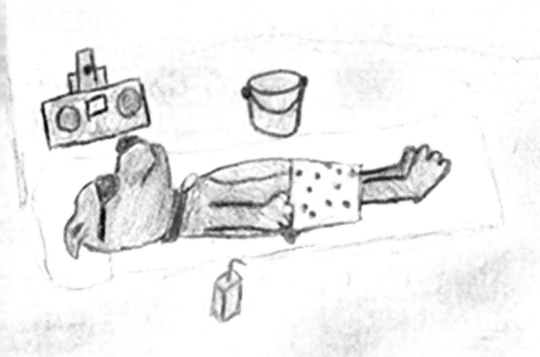

and lying in the sun.

Jinx said, "Come play with us...
we could use more friends for this game."

"I'm Jinx, and this is Lanky.
What is your name?"

Made in the USA
San Bernardino, CA
10 February 2014